MW01012928

Every Cowgirl
Goes to School

REBECCA JANNI ★ ILLUSTRATIONS BY LYNNE AVRIL

DIAL BOOKS FOR YOUNG READERS ★ AN IMPRINT OF PENGUIN GROUP (USA) INC.

To Mom, my first and best teacher

Acknowledgment:
With special thanks to Mrs. Strand and
all the teachers who touch lives every day.

—R.J.

To my teachers all through school, and to all teachers everywhere,
who give so much to the next generation of kids
—L.A.

DIAL BOOKS FOR YOUNG READERS · A division of Penguin Young Readers Group
Published by The Penguin Group ✶ Penguin Group (USA) Inc., 375 Hudson Street, New York, NY 10014, U.S.A. ✶ Penguin Group (Canada), 90
Eglinton Avenue East, Suite 700, Toronto, Ontario, Canada M4P 2Y3 (a division of Pearson Penguin Canada Inc.) ✶ Penguin Books Ltd, 80
Strand, London WC2R 0RL, England ✶ Penguin Ireland, 25 St. Stephen's Green, Dublin 2, Ireland (a division of Penguin Books Ltd) ✶ Penguin
Group (Australia), 707 Collins Street, Melbourne, Victoria 3008, Australia ✶ (a division of Pearson Australia Group Pty Ltd) ✶ Penguin Books
India Pvt Ltd, 11 Community Centre, Panchsheel Park, New Delhi - 110 017, India ✶ Penguin Group (NZ), 67 Apollo Drive, Rosedale, Auckland
0632, New Zealand (a division of Pearson New Zealand Ltd) ✶ Penguin Books (South Africa), Rosebank Office Park, 181 Jan Smuts Ave,
Parktown North 2193, South Africa ✶ Penguin China, B7 Jiaming Center, 27 East Third Ring Road North, Chaoyang District, Beijing 100020,
China ✶ Penguin Books Ltd, Registered Offices: 80 Strand, London WC2R 0RL, England

Text copyright © 2013 by Rebecca Janni ✶ Illustrations copyright © 2013 by Lynne Avril. All rights reserved.

The publisher does not have any control over and does not assume any responsibility for author or third-party websites or their content.

Designed by Irene Vandervoort and Jasmin Rubero ✶ Text set in Tweed Md ✶ Manufactured in China on acid-free paper

10 9 8 7 6 5 4 3 2 1

Library of Congress Cataloging-in-Publication Data
Janni, Rebecca.
Every cowgirl goes to school / by Rebecca Janni ; illustrated by Lynne Avril.
p. cm.
Summary: From having to leave her cowgirl hat at home to being seated between the
rambunctious "J-twins," a brand-new day in a brand-new class is not going Nellie Sue's
way, especially with her best friend, Anna, being nice to new girl Maya.
ISBN 978-0-8037-3937-6 (hardcover)
[1. Cowgirls—Fiction. 2. First day of school—Fiction. 3. Schools—Fiction. 4. Friendship—Fiction.]
I. Avril, Lynne, date, ill. II. Title.
PZ7.J2436Eug 2013   [E]—dc23   2012021666

The artwork was done in watercolor and gouache with an ink outline.

It was a brand-new class and a brand-new day, and I had it all planned out. Mrs. Clark even sent me a letter and a paper bag to fill with five things about me for show-and-tell.

GOAt Wrangler

What's in the bag?
Do you want to see?
FIVE special things
All about ME!

I stuffed the bag in my backpack and grabbed my cowgirl hat. "Sorry," Mama said. "No hats at school. It's a rule."

The bus pulled up and I looked for my friend Anna, but she was already on board. Ginger tried to climb on, too, but Mama held her back. No dogs on the bus. It's a rule.

All the seats were full except one.

"Looks like someone got a front row seat," said Drivin' Ivan.

Mrs. Moore squished in beside me and practically sat on my lap.

I peeked over my backpack and saw Anna talking with some girl.

At school, Anna told me, "I wanted to save you a spot, but everything was taken. Maya here made room for me. She's new at our school."

"Hello," Maya said in a voice like bells.

"How-dee, Pardner!"

"No," she said. "My name's Maya."

"Well, hi-ya, Maya!"

Mrs. Clark had a place for everything. Lockers for backpacks, a cooler for lunch bags, and desks for the kids. Anna and Maya were right in the middle of the room, but I couldn't find my name anywhere.

My desk was in the far back corner,
between the J-twins, Jacob and Joshua,
who were wrestling over a purple marker.
This brand-new day was not goin' my way.

After morning announcements, we pledged our allegiance and sang the good morning song.

I started to strum my air guitar, and the J-twins joined in. Mrs. Clark folded her arms and I froze like a popsicle. Maya whispered something in Anna's ear, and they both laughed.

In story time, we read about a bunch of animals
going back to school. The J-twins thought they
were dogs, and I had to get away from their drool.
I bumped into Maya, and she gave me a look.

Then it was time for PE.

Mr. Crabtree said, "Only tennis shoes on the gym floor. School rules."

I pulled off my cowgirl boots, and a kickball flew over and hit me in the leg.

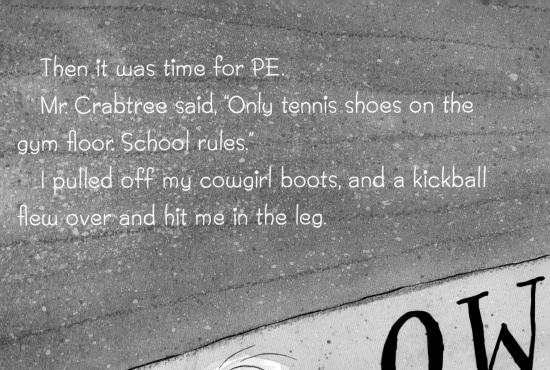

OW!

What do folks have against a good pair of boots? If soccer players wore 'em, they wouldn't need shin guards.

When PE was over, I had to go straight to recess in those tennis shoes. Anna and I were walking together, but Maya squeezed between us like a hound under a fence. She stepped on my shoelace and sent me flying. I landed in the playground pit and got a mouthful of sand.

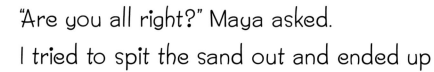

"Are you all right?" Maya asked.

I tried to spit the sand out and ended up
spitting right on Maya's foot.

"My new shoes!" she cried.

This brand-new day was NOT going my way.

Then, the lunch bell rang.

Lunch tasted kind of gritty with the leftover sand in my mouth.

I washed it down the best I could with a carton of milk.

Maya finished early and went back to class.

"She's nice, don't you think?" asked Anna.

I just took another drink.

When Anna and I got back to class,
there was a surprise on my desk.
A picture of me . . .

... looking like a cow.

"Look," Maya said, "you make such a pretty cow."

The whole class gathered around to see,
and I could feel my face turning redder than
Mama's tomatoes.
The J-twins started to *moo*, and then
others joined in.

No shoes could get me out of there
fast enough. I ran down the hall.

This brand-new day was NOT going my way!

A voice behind me said, "I didn't mean to hurt your feelings. I drew the picture because Anna told me you were a cowgirl, and I thought cowgirls loved cows. Please come back, Nellie Sue. I want to be your friend. Besides it's time for the all-about-me bags."

Suddenly I felt bad for not
showing her enough cowgirl hospitality.
I took her hand, and we walked back to class together.

When we got back, Maya started to crumple up the cow poster.

"Wait," I said. "Can I have it?"

"Sure," she said. "I made it for you."

In class, Mrs. Clark handed us our all-about-me bags.
Anna stood in front of the class and showed us
her ballet slippers and sparkly tiara.

Maya shared a piano recital ribbon and a soccer trophy.

The J-twins got their bags mixed up and started wrestling again.

When it was my turn,
I lined up my things on the table . . .

my picture of good old Beauty,
my two-wheeled horse,

Ginger's favorite tennis ball,

a Miley Smiley CD,

MILEY-SMILEY HITS

a homemade blue ribbon
I got for catching a goat, and . . .

#1

GOAt Wrangler

the cow poster my new friend gave me.
Maya smiled.

The J-twins started to *moo* again.

I looked at them and said, "I'm glad
you know your animal sounds,"
and they got real quiet.

It was a brand-new day, and I decided
it would go just my way.